HEY
JUDE

HEY JUDE

Star Spider

orca soundings

ORCA BOOK PUBLISHERS

Published in Canada and the United States in 2020 by Orca Book Publishers.
orcabook.com

Library and Archives Canada Cataloguing in Publication
Title: Hey Jude / Star Spider.
Names: Spider, Star, author.
Series: Orca soundings.
Description: Series statement: Orca soundings
Identifiers: Canadiana (print) 2020017603X | Canadiana (ebook) 20200176048 |
ISBN 9781459826359 (SOFTCOVER) | ISBN 9781459826366 (PDF) |
ISBN 9781459826373 (EPUB)
Classification: LCC PS8637.P54 H49 2020 | DDC jc813/.6—dc23

Library of Congress Control Number: 2020930589

Summary: In this high-interest accessible novel for teen readers,
a teen tries to balance the last year of high school, a new romance
and looking after her sister with mental health issues.

Orca Book Publishers is committed to reducing the consumption
of nonrenewable resources in the making of our books. We make
every effort to use materials that support a sustainable future.

Orca Book Publishers gratefully acknowledges the support for its
publishing programs provided by the following agencies: the Government
of Canada, the Canada Council for the Arts and the Province of British
Columbia through the BC Arts Council and the Book Publishing Tax Credit.

Edited by Tanya Trafford
Design by Ella Collier
Cover images by Gettyimages.ca/pixhook (front) and
Shutterstock.com/Krasovski Dmitri (back)

Printed and bound in Canada.

23 22 21 20 • 1 2 3 4

To Ben, for always

taking care.

Chapter One

It's the first day of school. Jude doesn't answer when I call her down to breakfast. My heart seizes up briefly, but I manage to breathe through it. I call her one more time before I abandon my lumpy effort at pancakes and run upstairs. As I make my way down the hall, I try hard to convince myself that everything is fine. She's probably just playing music or something and can't hear me. I listen at her door.

No music. I knock quietly. No response. I exhale to steady myself and push the door open. I took the lock off her door a year ago, when she had a bad episode. Really bad. Which is why I get so panicky. I'm always wondering when it's going to happen again.

The first thing that hits me is the smell. People say teenage girls smell like sugar and spice and everything nice, but that's total bullshit. Jude smells as bad as a teenage boy. And to make matters worse, she tries to hide it by applying a toxic level of scented lotion to her body after she showers. It's truly awful.

Jude's room is dark. The floor is covered in a thick layer of clothes, magazines and crumpled paper. Not a good sign. I wade through the mess and pull up her blackout blinds, which are coated in a nasty layer of dust. How long has it been since I've been in here? She usually keeps the door closed and is pretty particular about her privacy, but I shouldn't have let it get this bad. I usually make weekly checks. But I've let it slide because I've been so busy with my summer job at Java World. Someone has to help Mom. She works hard, but there is never quite enough to cover the bills.

The light from the morning sun streams through the window, making all the dust I've kicked up way too visible. I unlock the window and throw it open. It doesn't help much.

I pick up one of the crumpled pieces of paper and open it up. It's a face, so scratched out that the original drawing is barely visible. Another bad sign. Jude only hates her art like this when she's starting to crash.

As I make my way to the bed, I move carefully, trying to avoid stepping on anything. The comforter is pulled so high I can't even see Jude's head. I sit down on the side of the bed and something crunches under me. I don't even bother checking to see what it is. Instead I pull back the covers to reveal my sister, a lump of arms and hair with no face.

She groans, low and long, and rolls over.

"Hey, Jude," I say quietly. It's our little family joke. My mom was a Beatles fanatic back in the day, so she named her daughters Penny and Jude. Kind of embarrassing when people make the connection. Luckily it doesn't happen that often. Most people our age are clueless about music from older generations.

Jude groans again, this time more of a grunt. "Fuck off, Penny Lane," she says.

I'm used to her sass, but that doesn't mean it doesn't sting. I reach out and touch her shoulder, give her a little shake. "First day of school, kiddo. I'm making pancakes."

"Your pancakes suck," she mutters.

I roll my eyes, which doesn't matter because she can't see me.

But she's right. For some reason I have never been able to make good pancakes. I'm a master of all the other breakfast foods. Eggs, oatmeal, even omelets, but pancakes are my mortal enemy. They're always lumpy or way too flat. I continue to do battle with them though. I'm determined. It's kind of my thing.

"Seriously, Jude, tenth grade, first day," I say.

Jude's two years younger than me. I'm already worrying about what she'll do if I decide to go to university. Mom works nights at the hospital as a nurse and sleeps all day, so who will wake Jude up in the mornings? Cook her horrible pancakes? Most important, who will be there when she crashes?

"First day can live without me. I'm too tired." She rolls over to face me but doesn't move the hair out of her face.

I bend over to try to see her eyes through the mass of tangled brown.

"Then we have to up your meds," I reply.

She pushes the hair out of her face finally and glares at me. She's pale. Too pale. I try to keep my concern tucked away behind a relaxed mask. She can read me too well. I don't want her to feel like something is wrong. That will probably just make things worse.

"I know it's not ideal, but that's what the doctor said," I say. "Here." I dig her first dose of the day out of my pocket and hand it to her. It's part of my morning ritual—get Jude's drugs, shower, eat breakfast, brush my teeth. "I'll get you another pill to take with the pancakes."

She groans again but swallows the pills, then opens her mouth wide to prove it.

This is our deal. About a year ago she almost died from an overdose. One morning she didn't respond to me when I called, and I had to kick down her door. I found her passed out with an empty bottle of meds next to her. I had to shove my finger down her throat and make her puke them up before calling 9-1-1. So now we have a deal. I make sure she gets up, eats my shitty pancakes and takes her pills. And for nearly a year we have been good. So good that Mom thinks everything is fine now. I know better, but I don't want to worry her. I hope this is just a single bad day, though, not the beginning of a downward spiral.

I'll have to keep a closer eye on her. And make her clean her room.

I get up, remove the granola-bar wrapper stuck to my ass and wipe off the crumbs. I crumple the wrapper into a tiny ball and stick it in my pocket.

"Down in five. And tonight you clean your room."

Jude has pulled her hair back from her face now. She smiles at me sarcastically. She's way, way prettier than me. But I've never had time to be jealous.

"Okay, Penny Lane, you're the boss," she says in a singsong voice.

"That's right," I reply. "I am."

Chapter Two

For most people, the first day of school is something to dread. But not for me. I'm a good student, and I love the structure of school. It's all laid out for you, and people tell you what to do. It's a huge change from the rest of my life. Taking care of Jude, for one—always telling her what to do and making sure she follows the rules. Plus, I'm a manager at Java World, and I have to boss people around there too. So school is a dream. I don't even mind when teachers are assholes. I just smile sweetly and get my work done.

Jude and I ride the subway together and head to the same place, but technically she goes to a different school. The alternative school is located in the same building as my public school. It's a place people go when they don't quite fit in regular school. When they need extra help, looser rules, more time with the teachers. It's amazing, actually, because Jude gets to focus on her art there. I've met most of her teachers, and they are good people, way less burned out than mine. I thought about going there myself. But it would be much harder to graduate with all the "extras" I need for my applications for grants and loans for university.

When we climb out of the subway station and step out into the city streets, there's a bit of a breeze. It's a relief. I'm not much into the heat, so I can't wait to be done with summer. Fall is my absolute favorite. I love the colors, the smell of dying leaves and bonfires, the back-to-school excitement.

I look over at Jude. Her eyes are only half-open, and she's walking so slowly. I fed her the extra pill this morning, and I pray it will kick in soon. I had to scrap the pancakes—they were just too terrible. So we ate slightly stale Froot Loops instead. We always have them in the house because they're Jude's favorite. Sometimes I like to let her have things she loves because most of the time I'm just ordering her to do stuff she hates.

Jude grabs my hand as we approach the front door of the school. We have done this every first day of school since I was old enough to take her on my own. It's a little ritual we have that I love. Today it makes me even more happy—hopefully it's a sign that she hasn't crashed too hard. I squeeze her hand tightly even though it's so warm out that both of our hands are nasty and sweaty.

I walk her to the entrance of her school. There's a big mural over the door. The art class makes one at the end of every year for the incoming students.

It's bright and colorful, decorated with rainbows, smiling faces, mountain ranges and various sketches of people doing art—bent over drawings, writing on old-fashioned typewriters, carving sculptures. I love the sketches the most, but I'm biased. Most of them are Jude's. She's incredibly talented and creates such beautiful work when she's not depressed.

Jude turns to me. Her face is serious and lovely in the morning light and reminds me of her self-portraits. She often draws them—I have a million tacked to the walls of my bedroom. Somehow she always manages to capture her own stunning sadness. That look in her eyes like she has seen worse things than I can ever imagine. And still she keeps getting up every morning.

"You know I love you, right, Penny Lane?" she asks.

I nod, my eyes burning with tears that I try hard to contain.

"Hey, Jude," I whisper, "I love you too."

"Have a good year," she replies. She puts her hands on my cheeks and leans in to kiss me lightly on the forehead. It's a fleeting thing, the kiss, but it is heavy with all the things she doesn't say but I know she really feels.

Then she's gone.

I watch her as she moves away, her feet dragging a bit too much. As fragile and pale as a dream.

"You too," I call out. The words that finish our ritual, break the spell.

She doesn't turn around. She just raises her hand and waves. I'm dismissed. Allowed, for now, to go about my own life and enjoy the small thrill of a new school year.

Chapter Three

Most people have already gone in. I heard the first bell when I was seeing Jude off, but I know I still have a couple of minutes before the second bell. It doesn't really matter anyway, though, because it's my final year and most of my teachers know me well. I have a certain degree of freedom. They know about Jude and the complications of being her caregiver and trust me to get my work done. So I take this time to wander down the halls without hurrying. I run my fingers along the lockers, feeling the cold metal and listening to the sound of the locks shifting under my touch. I love that sound. The smell is wonderful too— pencil shavings and fresh paper, with an occasional whiff of body spray.

The halls are deserted, so it comes as a complete shock when I round the corner and almost run into someone. We both stop short. He smiles. I have never seen this boy before. He has the whitest, straightest teeth I have ever seen. His dark brown skin and closely shaved hair highlight the spiky red mohawk that runs all the way down to the back of his neck. He's wearing dress pants with suspenders and a Beatles T-shirt, *Yellow Submarine*, which just happens to be my favorite album. And his gray eyes are lined with just the slightest hint of black liner.

I have no words.

I smile back at him and then immediately flush with embarrassment.

"Hi," he says. His voice is low but delicate, like he's not quite used to the sound of it.

"Hi," I reply. I'm surprised I can even say that much. I'm not much for dating, because Jude takes up so much of my time. But it's not like I'm a robot. This guy is *hot*.

"I'm looking for B101," he says.

"You're new," I say, then shut my mouth quickly. What a stupid thing to say. Of course he's new. I *definitely* would have noticed him last year.

"Is it that obvious?" he says. He spreads his arms, palms up, and looks down at himself.

I laugh, but it comes out more like a bark. I smile to try to cover it up. He tilts his head at me and looks puzzled.

"Actually, I'm going to B101 right now," I say.

The second bell rings. It's so loud we both cover our ears. I'm usually in the classroom by second bell, so I'm not used to the volume of it bouncing around the empty halls.

"Physics?" he asks after the bell has finished.

"My favorite," I reply. I try to sound like I'm joking, but it comes out completely serious. I mean, I wasn't joking—I do love physics. But I was trying to keep it light in case he hates it and thinks I'm a giant nerd.

"I'm more into chemistry," he replies, "but it's all physics in the end, isn't it?"

I wait for a second to make sure he's not joking. But his smile is sincere. Have I died and gone to heaven?

"Yeah," I say. "I mean, I guess."

There's a moment of silence where we just stare at each other.

"So?" he asks, raising his eyebrows.

"What?"

"The classroom?"

"The class..." My brain is definitely not working.

"Like, where we sit in desks, write notes and listen to the teacher drone on about velocity?"

My eyes keep venturing down to his lips. It's hard to focus on the words he's saying. It takes me a second to snap out of it.

"The classroom. Yes." I start walking abruptly and almost bump into him. I'm not usually like this, I swear. But I can't seem to control the feeling that's pulsing though me. The boy with the funky hair and perfect smile turns to follow me. I notice that he has an earthy boy smell. I like it.

"I'm Jack, by the way," he says as we head toward the classroom.

"Jack," I say. "Cool. I'm Penny."

"Like Penny Lane?" he asks, laughing a little.

I look over my shoulder at him. He's walking slightly behind me but still keeping up. He locks eyes with me, and it makes me shiver. His gray eyes stand out against his dark brown skin. I've never seen eyes like his before.

"Yeah, actually," I reply.

His eyes open a little wider, and I feel like I could just fall right into them.

"Really? That's cool. I'm a fan, if you couldn't tell." He points to his T-shirt.

"I love *Yellow Submarine*," I say.

"Yeah, me too."

I look forward again just in time to see the door of B101. It would be just like me to miss it completely and make an even bigger ass of myself. I stop suddenly, and he bumps into me. We both laugh, and I point at the door.

"Classroom," I say.

He grins at me. "Classroom, good," he says like a caveman.

I laugh a little too loudly as he opens the door and waves me inside.

Chapter Four

I stare at Jack way too much during physics class. He catches me a couple of times and smiles, like it's completely normal to have some girl he barely knows watching him. Whenever I try to look away, something always brings me back. It's not that I've never felt this way about someone before. But it's been a long time, and I feel a little embarrassed by my instant attraction. For me crushes can be kind of annoying and distracting. They are too overwhelming. Too many hormones pounding through my bloodstream, making me giddy and unable to focus. And I have too much going on to lose focus. I can't afford to waste my time staring at someone for an entire class.

By the time the bell rings, I've managed to pull my attention back to work. I quickly whip through the exercises and write down the homework assignment. I mean, it's the bare minimum, but it will have to do for now. On the way out I slow down because I can see that Jack is still packing up. I'm hoping our paths will cross again. I even go so far as to drop my notebook, a totally obvious move. But it works. Jack falls into step next to me just as I get out into the hall.

"How was class?" he asks. He sounds a bit cheeky. He probably knows exactly how class was, with me staring at him the whole time. He's just trying to bug me.

I flush and shrug. "Good," I manage to say.

He runs his hand through his mohawk, and I try not to wish it was my hands in his hair.

"So I'm new…" he says, his words drifting off.

"We did establish that," I reply. I meant it to sound joking, but it comes out a little bitchy. He laughs nervously, and I instantly feel bad.

"Well, yeah, so I'm wondering if you wanted to show me around?"

I want that more than anything, but I have another class to get to. Then I have to meet Jude for lunch in the pit. The pit is the gross, slightly indented dirt area behind the school where most of the upper-grade kids go to smoke and eat lunch. Jude and I have a picnic table that we have claimed as our own. It's the place we always meet, sometimes with a couple of other friends, to check in.

"Sorry, I've got to get to class," I say, pointing down the hall. English is next. "And I have to meet my sister at lunch."

"Oh, yeah, me too. Get to class, I mean," Jack says.

"But you could join us, if you want, for lunch? At the pit?" I finally risk looking over at him. I had been trying to avoid doing that because I know the look on my face will give my feelings away.

"The pit?" He raises his eyebrows in the most adorable way.

I want to reach out and grab him and drag him to a dark corner to make out. But I take a deep breath and restrain myself like a champ.

"Yeah, it's behind the school. Kind of nasty, like a giant ashtray."

He laughs. I look down the hall toward my English class. I'm kind of tempted to ask him to skip with me. But I've never skipped a class in my whole high-school career, and I can't afford to start now.

"Anyway, lunchtime. The pit. I'll be there."

"Cool. Yeah. Sounds good," he replies.

It hurts to pull myself away from him. As I walk toward my class, my brain starts to whirl. What the hell am I thinking? This is the first day of my final year. I have to focus if I want to keep up my grades and get the scholarships I so desperately need. I can't do the getting-distracted-by-hormones thing. I'm better than this. But the second I think about Jack's amazing gray eyes and lopsided smile, my good intentions fade. Damn it. I'm only one class into twelfth grade, and I am already screwed.

Chapter Five

I leave class early because I've finished the work Mr. Sandeep assigned. I've had him as a teacher before. I've loved him since ninth grade and have even switched classes a couple of times so I could have him as my teacher.

The first day is always the same. He asks us all for our input in building the reading list for the class.

He actually pays attention to what his students are interested in. I have some go-to favorites. I love the *Marrow Thieves* by Cherie Dimaline and *Son of a Trickster* by Eden Robinson. And modern plays are great, like Tompson Highway's *The Rez Sisters* and *A Raisin in the Sun*. Plus I love long-form poetry. Dante's *The Divine Comedy* has been one of my favorite poems since I first read it in grade ten (really). Today I try to switch it up so Mr. Sandeep knows I'm making an effort. I add in a couple of children's titles for good measure: *Alice in Wonderland* and *Charlotte's Web*. People think kid's books are shallow, but they can actually be really deep and meaningful.

The halls are empty as I head to my locker to grab my lunch and walk out to the pit. When I push through the back door of the school, I spot Jude immediately. She's sitting at our table. It's been made ours by the sheer amount of art Jude has carved into its surface. She's got her back to me, but I see a curl of smoke rising above her head. She's bent over, clearly concentrating hard on something. I feel a small swell of rage. She shouldn't be smoking. I've talked to her about this a million times. I march over and grab the cigarette out of her mouth, toss it to the ground and stomp on it. I'm so distracted by my anger I almost miss her quickly pulling her pant leg down and palming something that looks like a pen. I figured she had been drawing, or carving into the table again, but this is new.

She looks at me with narrowed eyes, then glances down at her smoke, crushed on the ground.

"Hi, Mom," she says with a sly smile. She always calls me that when I do something particularly Mom-ish. I hate it and love it at the same time.

"When did you start smoking again? Also, what the hell is that?" I make a grab for the hand she hid the pen in. She squeezes it shut, and I pry it open. It's definitely a pen, but it's been retrofitted with a needle on the end of it.

"What the fuck, Jude?" I ask. Then I go for her pant leg. Her reflexes aren't fast enough to catch me. I pull it up to reveal a fresh, still-bleeding blue tattoo of a phoenix. I open my mouth, then close it. It's beautiful obviously. All her art is perfect. But the tattoo looks painful, and the fact that she is using pen ink makes me want to puke.

"Jesus Christ, Jude! What's wrong with you?" I don't know what else to say. This is a whole new level for her. Although maybe it's not. On closer inspection, I can see that parts of the tattoo are not fresh. The blue is a bit worn and faded.

"Um, I'm fucking nuts?" Jude replies.

I shake my head. She promised me a long time ago that she wouldn't diminish her mental illness like that. She also promised she wouldn't use it as an excuse when she did stupid teenage shit.

I look down at the pen. I don't know what to do with it. It's clearly a biohazard.

Just then the lunch bell rings. I sigh.

"I mean, it's nice and everything," I say. "I mean, the phoenix, but pen ink isn't tattoo ink. It's toxic, horrible. So dangerous, Jude."

Jude shrugs, shakes her head and lies back on the bench. She stretches out like a cat and closes her eyes. She looks tired but still stunning. It breaks my heart that she might be crashing again. And it scares the crap out of me.

I look over all her drawings and carvings on the table as I hear the low murmur of people in the distance. Kids are pouring out of the school, talking, laughing, lighting smokes. Her drawings are amazing, some of them fragile, delicate, some of them sad and dark. Just like her. I want to support her art in any way I can. But I can't support her poisoning herself or piercing herself repeatedly without proper disinfectant.

"Um...hi?" I hear a familiar voice behind me.

I whip around and there is Jack, in all his mohawked, suspendered, *Yellow Submarine* T-shirted glory. I flash him a quick smile, and his eyes travel down to my hand. I'm still clutching the pen, and the needle is gleaming a little in the light.

"You making a shiv or something?" he asks, nodding at the pen.

"Nope, she's confiscating mine," Jude says from behind me. I turn to throw her a glare. She's sitting up now, her pant leg still rolled above her knee. It looks like she was studying the tattoo, but now her intense brown eyes are focused on Jack. My heart seizes. I didn't think this through. I've never had a real boyfriend or girlfriend that I brought home. Only occasional flings and definitely not at my house. So I never had to worry about Jude enchanting any of my crushes. But the way she's looking at Jack, like she's just been delivered a delicious meal, makes me want to melt into a sad puddle on the ground. Beautiful Jude, mysterious and temperamental. How could I ever compete?

Jack narrows his eyes at my sister. I see him taking in all of her. Her lush brown hair piled up in a perfectly messy bun. Her wide dark eyes outlined in charcoal black. Her full lips coated in deep crimson lipstick. She's a manic pixie dream girl, a vision. Beside her I am plain. But she's the most important person in my life, so that has never mattered. Until now.

I hold my breath.

"Cool tattoo," Jack says.

"She did it herself," I reply, my voice proud. Oh my god, why did I just say that? I'm so used to defending her and lifting her up. Making her feel good about herself when she's at her lowest. And now it's all coming back to bite me in the ass. I have just made her look a million times cooler in front of the one person I absolutely don't want her to impress.

Jude shrugs and smiles and stretches out on the bench again, arching her back seductively. I feel light-headed watching her, knowing there is every possibility this will end any hope I had of catching Jack's attention.

But when I glance back at him, he's looking at me. His gray eyes catch mine, and a slow smile curls his lips. I'm in complete shock. His smile is for me.

"So how about that tour, Penny Lane?" he asks.

I finally let out the breath I've been holding this whole time.

Chapter Six

My school is just a school, so there's not really much to it. But obviously I try to drag out the tour with Jack for as long as I can. I'm painfully aware that it is pretty boring though. Especially compared with Jude's school next door, which has couches in most of the classrooms. And an art room that looks like a rainbow threw up all over the place. And a lounge/kitchen that doubles as an art gallery for all the students to show off their work. I start with the library. Then we hit the nurse's office, so I can dispose of Jude's tattoo pen properly. After that it's the theater, one of my favorite places to be. I'm not an actor, but I love watching plays, and the drama club performs at least two a year, written and directed by the kids. I've seen some pretty great stuff here.

The theater is empty, and there is nothing left on the "tour," so Jack and I spend the rest of lunch sitting on the stage, our feet dangling over the edge. I have leftovers from last night's dinner. Jack has cafeteria sushi, which is not amazing but better than most of the cafeteria food at least.

"So your sister seems nice," he says. He speaks quietly, but the acoustics in the theater are so good that his voice is magnified in an amazingly perfect way.

My heart clenches in my chest again. Is that what we're going to talk about? My sister?

"Nice isn't exactly the word I'd choose," I reply. "But she's fascinating for sure—enchanting even. When she's not sick, that is."

Did I seriously just say that? I'm such an asshole. It wasn't me opening up. I know that. It was me trying to sabotage Jude. Trying to break any hold she might have on Jack.

I look over at him. He doesn't look back at me. He's staring across the theater, and I wonder what he's thinking. I'm not usually this insecure. I usually move through the world with ease and confidence. That's what happens when your dad dies and your mom is tossed into working more than full-time to manage the debts he left behind. You grow up fast.

"Sick," he says.

It doesn't seem like a question, but I answer it anyway.

"She has depression. I mean, not all the time, but she has tried to kill herself a couple of times, and now I have to take care of her." I'm talking too much, too fast. And I'm starting to wonder if this is no longer me trying to sabotage Jude but actually me opening up. I don't do that much. I have a few friends, but they're mostly school friends. Nerds like me who are into talking about physics, history, philosophy, art. We go deep but usually not personal.

Jack looks over at me. His eyes are soft, unfocused. They're shining, even in the low light.

"Me too," he says.

I frown.

"I mean the trying-to-kill-myself part, not the taking-care-of-your-sister part. Obviously."

I'm shocked. I don't know what to say. I thought I was oversharing, but now here is this beautiful human right beside me willing to tell me something so emotional, so real.

"I'm sorry," I whisper.

He leans over and nudges me with his shoulder. Cracks a smile. I feel warm where his arm made contact with mine.

"Don't look so sad about it," he says.

"But it's sad."

He shrugs. "It happens."

"But you're so...calm about it."

He laughs, and it sounds sincere. Its golden sound bounces around in the theater and comes back to me over and over. I never want to stop hearing it.

"I didn't come out of the box this way, trust me. It took a long time to get here."

I lean back on my hands and look up at the stage lights. I've never performed because I've never had time. But I've always wondered what it would be like. Makeup melting under all the hot lights. So many people looking at you, caught up in your story. You can't see the audience when you're standing in the glow of the stage lights. But I imagine you would know they were there. You would feel the electric pulse of all those eyes, all that attention.

"I'm not there yet," I say quietly. "Calm, I mean."

I can feel him looking at me. But I don't turn my head.

"I don't know where to put it, you know?" I continue.

Out of the corner of my eye, I see him nod. "There are groups, you know, for family members to...vent."

It's my turn to laugh. Between work and school and grocery shopping and cleaning the house, there's no time for groups. Or stage lights. Or love even.

After a minute I finally look over at him. His eyes are laser-focused on mine. It feels amazing to bask in his attention. His smile is sad, and for a second it reminds me of Jude—this sorrowful beauty.

I want to lean over and kiss the frown right off his lips. And there's a moment when I think it might happen. He raises his hand ever so slightly, like he's going to reach out and touch me. I move over a tiny bit. My mouth tingles with anticipation. But then the moment passes. Something behind his eyes snaps shut, and he suddenly jumps down off the stage. I stay seated, shocked at his quick change. Maybe I was just fooling myself? Moving too fast? Life has no slow setting for me.

"I have to go," he says, his voice a little gruff.

"Okay." I don't know what else to say.

"But here." Jack pulls out his phone, types in his code and passes it to me. "Punch in your number."

I smile, probably a little too hard. When I'm done typing, I hand the phone back to him, and our fingers touch. I shiver.

He smiles, but before I can say anything else he takes off. I watch him make his way up the aisle and out the main door of the theater.

For the first time in a long time, I wish that life really did have a slow setting.

Chapter Seven

The rest of the day is uneventful, mostly because I don't see Jack again. He doesn't text me either, so I have no way to contact him. I wish I had sent myself a test text from his phone so I would at least have his number. Not that I would know what to say. We were getting pretty personal there for a second, and then he just ran away. Maybe he already has a girlfriend? A boyfriend? Maybe I just read the whole situation totally wrong, and he didn't want to lead me on? Whatever it was, I try not to think about it, try to focus on my classes instead. It doesn't work though. Since this is the first day, there isn't much in the way of actual learning.

When Jude and I get home from school, my mom is awake. She's in cleaning mode, bustling around the house, tidying up. Jude's room certainly is the worst offender, but it's not the only problem. The house is almost always a cluttered nightmare. When I work full-time in the summer, it's even worse. And Jude is no help, of course.

Mom barely stops to greet us. Just buzzes by us in her old green robe, which smells a bit rank. Clean clothes are the hardest thing to come by in our house. The washer and dryer are so old that more than half of the time they don't work. And more than half of the time we don't have the money to get them repaired. I think it would be cheaper to buy new ones anyway. But that is way too much cash to spend all in one place. We're spread thin enough as it is.

Jude and I retreat to our rooms before dinner to work. At least, I'm working—prepping all my binders and class schedules, looking over my textbooks. Jude, however, is doing whatever Jude does.

When her schedule allows, Mom insists on making dinner and having us all sit down to enjoy the meal together. She never lets us help, even though I always offer to. When everything is ready, she rings a little bell to summon us. It's an age-old tradition that both Jude and I love.

After about an hour or so, I hear the bell ring. I knock on Jude's door as I pass by. I don't hear a response, though, so I open it and peek in. The room is pitch-black because the blinds are down again. I trudge quickly through the dank mess on her floor and pull them up. Then I move over to the bed, where Jude is completely buried in her comforter again. A repeat of this morning. Not a good sign. I peel back the blanket to reveal her face, serene and pale. She is sound asleep. I almost don't want to wake her.

But if I don't, Mom might know something's up and send her to the hospital. And I can't break my part of our bargain. Jude does what I say, takes her pills, lives her life, and I don't report her to Mom.

I shake her gently, and she moans. She cracks her eyes open and squints at me. Somehow her makeup is still perfect. Just like those women in the movies who wake up looking perfect and smudge-free.

"Go away, Mom," Jude hisses.

"The dinner bell rang, Jude," I reply. "Mom's expecting us. I can't keep my side of the deal if you don't."

She sighs, bulldozers over me and rolls out of bed. On the floor, she tries to free herself from her blanket with what seems like way too much effort. Then she stands and follows me out the door.

"And you *are* cleaning your room tonight," I say.

She sighs again but doesn't answer. I hate talking to her as if she's a child, but sometimes that's the only way I can get her to respond.

Mom has made us mock-chicken fingers, cheesy toast and a pile of steaming peas. It's a fairly uninteresting meal, but I try to look grateful. I became a vegetarian in fifth grade after watching a video about the meat industry. After that I refused to eat anything "with a face." Instead of making different meals for Jude and me, Mom just embraced my choice, and we all went veggie. I love that about her. She just rolls with whatever life hands her.

"So how did it go?" Mom asks, her mouth full of peas. She always eats super fast because she has to leave right after dinner to go to work. I hate that she has to work so much and always be in a rush.

"Penny's got a boyfriend," Jude says in her singsong voice.

I shoot her a glare. But I'm happy she was able to get herself to the table. And she's actually participating in our conversation.

"Oh, really?" Mom says, looking over at me.

I blush.

"He's hot," Jude says, laughing a little and pushing her peas around on her plate. She's a master of the redirect. I am well aware that she's not actually eating, just moving the food around to look like she is. I will make sure she gets something later if I have to.

"When do we get to meet him?" Mom asks, shoving another forkful of peas into her mouth.

"How about...never," I say.

"Oh come on, Penny Lane," Mom says in a pretend whine.

I roll my eyes.

"Yeah, Penny Lane, we never get to meet any of your lovers," Jude says.

I hate it when they gang up on me like this.

"Not fair that Jude got to meet him and I didn't," Mom says, now putting on an expert pout.

"Okay, enough," I say. I haven't even eaten half of my meal, but I'm already pushing it away too. My stomach gets in knots when I think about Jack.

Mom frowns and reaches out to me. She squeezes my hand. "We were just joking, my love," she says.

I frown at her. She makes her most sincere *I love you* face. I can't help but let a single corner of my mouth turn up.

"He is pretty cute," I whisper.

Mom claps and goes back to her peas.

"Tell me everything," she says.

Chapter Eight

Mom's doing a double shift, so she'll have to sleep when she can at the hospital. As she gets her shoes on, I tell her again that I hate how she has to work so much. She grabs my cheeks and kisses me on the forehead.

"I do it because I love you two. You are my dream girls, you got that?"

All I can do is smile and hug her tightly.

Once Mom is out the door, I leave Jude in the kitchen to clean up. I go to my room to grab her night dose from my lockbox. I bought the box after she tried to overdose. It was expensive as hell, but worth it. I type in the four-number code and pop the door open. Jude's on a couple of different things. It's a complex mix of antidepressants and mood stabilizers that she and her psychiatrist worked out the first time she tried to kill herself. I have detailed instructions on how flexible we can be with the dosage. I have to be extra careful about raising it. Sometimes if a person is too depressed, a little bit of a boost from meds can increase the risk of suicide. It's like the brain hasn't caught up with itself— if there are thoughts of suicide in there already, having even a bit more energy can drive someone to complete. That's what they call it. Completing. Not succeeding, because that sounds too positive. It's a whole world of new language I had to learn quickly the hard way.

When I go back downstairs, Jude is gone. She didn't clean up.

"Hey, Jude!" I call up the stairs. "You better be cleaning your room."

I hear a slight groan from the general direction of her bedroom, so at least I know she's up there doing something. I sigh and tuck her pills into my pocket. Then I do a quick sweep of the kitchen. The dishwasher's been dead for two years, so I have to wash everything by hand. I like washing dishes though. It's sort of meditative, gives me time to think. Of course, my thoughts lead me to Jack. He still hasn't texted. I work through our conversation in the theater again. For the millionth time. My selfishness at outing Jude. That pressing desire to talk to someone about it. Jack's brave admission about his own mental health. The feeling of his shoulder on mine. I shiver despite the heat of the soapy water. I wish he would text. He ran away so quickly, and I want to know why. I want to know more about him in general. Where he came from, why he transferred, what music he likes besides the Beatles.

Once I'm done doing the dishes, I fill a glass with water to bring to Jude. Her door is slightly ajar, which is kind of weird. I peer in through the crack, but I can't see her. I push the door open with my foot.

"Here comes the airplane," I say to announce myself. I used to say that all the time when I was feeding her back when she was younger. I still say it sometimes now when I bring her pills. It's stupid, but it makes her laugh.

She doesn't respond. She's lying on her unmade bed, head down on a sketchbook, eyes closed. I'm surprised to see that she has actually cleaned up a little—if you can call heaping all the clothes and papers into a huge pile near her desk cleaning up.

I go over and sit down beside her.

"Jude," I say, giving her a little poke with my finger.

Her eyes shoot open, and her mouth makes a little round O.

"Sorry," I say. "I didn't mean to scare you."

She looks at me for a second like she doesn't know who I am. Then her confusion clears, and she frowns a little. I dig her pills out of my pocket and pass them to her with the glass of water. She looks down at the pills in her hand, and the frown deepens.

"Open wide," I say.

She pops the pills, opens her mouth for me, then picks up her sketchbook. It's another self-portrait, but the eyes are scratched out. She's gone over and over them with a black pen, covering them with little x's. It makes me sad—and scared. I stand up so I don't have to look at it. I walk over to the pile of clothes and crap by her desk and start pulling it apart piece by piece. I give every item the smell test except for the socks and underwear. I fold the clean clothes and toss the dirty ones into her laundry basket.

"Don't you ever get tired?" she asks, not looking up from her sketchbook, which she is now scribbling in.

I keep folding and tossing. Every once in a while I encounter a crumpled magazine or piece of paper in the pile. I uncrumple them and put them on her desk.

"Of what?" I ask. I know it's a leading question. Of course I get tired—everyone does. But I want to see what she means. I'm on high alert.

"Of living," she says.

I turn, and she looks up at me. Her makeup is still perfect. Did she reapply it at some point between sleeping and sleeping?

"Not cool, Jude," I say sternly. My Mom voice.

"You know what I mean." She rolls her eyes and tosses her sketchbook at me. I catch it but avoid looking at the picture of her with the dead x eyes. I close the book instead and put it on the growing pile on her desk.

Then I sigh. "Of course I do."

"You work so fucking hard. And for what?" she asks, her voice sharp.

I hate when she gets like this. Questions my entire existence just because she's questioning hers.

"For you, for Mom, for life," I reply.

Jude digs herself deeper under the comforter. "It's all just so exhausting."

"I know," I say. But I whisper it. I never want to make her feel like a burden.

Then I hear my phone ring, and my heart skips with excitement. I am so sure it's Jack that I can barely stop myself from running at top speed to my room.

It's not him though. It's my boss, calling me into work because one of my co-workers, Becky, just broke up with her boyfriend and won't stop crying into everyone's lattes. Now I have to close. Damn it.

I quickly get myself ready for my shift. When I check on Jude before I leave, she's asleep again. I always hate going out when she gets like this, but I don't have a choice.

Chapter Nine

The good news is that Jack texts me just as I step out the door. The bad news is he wants to go for a walk. But I'm on my way to work. He asks where I work, and I'm almost embarrassed to tell him. Java World is kind of gross, and a lot of the regulars are a little scummy. I mean, they're nice enough, but it ain't no Starbucks.

When I get there, my boss, Manny, is losing his shit. He's all alone, and there is a long line of customers waiting to order. I jump right in before I even put on my Java World T-shirt. Manny looks grateful and offers me one of his weird, over-the-top salesperson smiles. We deal with the line quickly. As soon as it's gone, he tells me he's got to run. His wife is pissed that he's not home because she has book club at their house, and he was supposed to take their three-year-old out for dinner and a movie. I wave him off, and he tells me I can keep all the tips for today. A whopping $5.33—I'm rich.

After the rush, things settle down and I get into a rhythm. A couple of regulars come in. Zane, an old guy who is missing all of his teeth, and Miss Pringle, who used to be a schoolteacher. Now she just teaches her cats how to fetch her things from the kitchen. I don't really believe her claims that they can actually open the fridge and get her a pop. But hey, you never know.

I start closing up a little earlier than Manny likes. He insists that we don't shut down until 9:00 p.m. on the dot, in case of last-minute latte orders. But I want to get out of here right at nine. I don't feel bad about it, because I always clean everything more thoroughly than any of my coworkers do. I usually find hidden grime that Becky or Abid left behind.

The bell on the door rings when I'm in the back, elbow deep in dishwater. My heart sinks. I'm washing the espresso machine, which I have already dismantled. I hate to say no to a customer, but there is not much else I can do. Maybe I'll get lucky and they'll just want a tea. I dry my arms and push through the kitchen curtain to the front.

And there is Jack. Looking hot and amazing and perfect, leaning against my counter, at my shitty little job.

He grins at me. "Still want that walk?"

I nod.

"Can I get a drink?" he says, flashing a five-dollar bill at me.

"What do you want?" I ask.

"Latte?"

I start to laugh, a bit more than makes sense. I suddenly realize how exhausted I am. I sink onto the stool beside the cash. Jack raises his eyebrows, those gray eyes of his sparkling.

"What's so funny?" he asks.

"I just shut down the machine."

"Ah, well, I'll just get myself a tea then, shall I?" He doesn't wait for an answer. He just walks around the counter and fixes it himself. Luckily there's no one left in the shop to report me to Manny. So I relax and watch Jack work. He looks confident behind the counter. He must have worked in a coffee shop before. He grabs a green-tea bag and fills the mug from the hot-water canister. Then he throws on a lid and grabs a cup sleeve. It takes him less than a minute. Then he's back around the other side of the counter, sticking the five-dollar bill into my tip jar. I laugh, and he winks at me.

"Fifteen minutes, okay?" I ask.

"Take all the time you need," he replies.

Twenty minutes later we are out on the street. He offers to walk me home. Usually I take the bus, but I'm happy for the fresh air. It's still warm, but the night has a hint of fall in it. I breathe deep and smile. Soon the leaves will start to turn, and then they will crunch under my feet. That is my favorite feeling in the world.

"So have you lived in the city your whole life?" Jack asks.

I nod, sipping on the hot chocolate I made myself before I left. It's too hot, and it burns the tip of my tongue.

"I'm guessing you didn't?" I ask.

He shoots me a look. "Do I have *hick* written all over me?"

I laugh. *Hick* is the last word I would *ever* use to describe him.

"I lived here in the city originally, but my parents moved us out to this small town in the middle of nowhere when I was, like, ten," he says. "What they called country paradise. There was a church there they were a part of, but that was about it for socializing. I had to be bused away to a bigger town for school. And let's just say that the diversity level was not that high. It sucked."

"Ugh, sorry," I say. "So your parents moved back here then?"

"Well, I did." There's a sadness in his voice.

I glance over at him. He's looking up at the sky, at the buildings around us. He's got this innocent expression on his face, like all this is new to him.

"They just let you go?" I ask.

"They made me," he replies.

I don't know what to say to that, so I stay quiet. I want to know more, but I don't want to pry.

"My big brother took me in. He's, like, eight years older than me. He's set up properly, sweet loft and everything. But I still feel like I'm intruding."

"That's rough," I say.

He shrugs. "Could be worse."

I laugh. "I guess it could always be worse."

"And what about you, Penny Lane?"

"What about me?"

We glance at each other and lock eyes. There's an intense interest in his gaze that I never see when people are looking at me. It makes me feel like I'm the center of the universe. A warm sensation that's not only the hot chocolate fills my stomach, and I smile.

"I'm just trying to exist," I say finally. "You know, keep my shit together."

"I never said it earlier, but I'm sorry about your sister," he says.

I shrug. Try to look casual. But my constant worry is eating me up.

"I love her to the ends of the earth," I say. Tears well in my eyes, and I blink them back. I pick up the pace. I need to get home and check on her. I texted her before I left work, but she didn't text back. She's probably just sleeping, but still.

Jack matches my pace. "Then she's the luckiest

person on earth," he says.

I stop in my tracks. Nobody has said anything that sweet to me in a long time. I turn to him, and he smiles.

"What?"

"It's just…you are so nice. Why are you so nice?"

"I'm just a small-town boy," he says with a bit of a twang in his voice. He holds up his hands innocently, and I want to grab them, put them around my waist. I step closer to him, inhale his earthy scent. He looks at me intensely for a long moment, his gaze slowly traveling to my lips. My skin feels electric. Then he frowns suddenly and pulls out his phone.

He checks it, but as it lights up I can see there aren't any messages. He quickly clicks it off and sticks it back in his pocket.

"Sorry, I have to go. I forgot that I have to get to the store and grab a few things for my brother before it closes."

"Oh," I say.

He shoots me a smile that I swear is a little sad, then gives me a wave and turns on his heel. I watch him walk away, a sinking feeling in my stomach. Was it me? His brother clearly didn't text, so what was that all about? He did the same thing at the theater. I wish I knew him well enough to just straight-out ask, but I don't want to pry.

He doesn't look back, and I wish he would.

Chapter Ten

After Jack leaves I walk home slowly. I want to give myself time to think and take in the air, which is getting cooler by the minute. But even at the slower pace, I soon reach my front door. Life is so fast for me. I wish I was more capable of slowing down and relaxing into things. Maybe that's why Jack keeps leaving so abruptly—he can sense that I always feel rushed.

When I get into the house, I putter around the kitchen for a bit to burn off my last bit of nervous energy. Then I climb the stairs. I don't go to my room though. Instead I sneak into Jude's. She's still buried under her comforter. But she hasn't closed the blinds, so the room is flooded in orange light from the streetlight outside her window. It gives the whole place a sullen sort of glow.

I finish sorting out her pile of laundry and papers. I'm not worried about waking her. When she's crashing, not even an elephant stomping through the room would disturb her. I would have to actually touch her to wake her up. When I'm done with the pile, I move on to the rest of the room. I start dusting everything with a T-shirt from her laundry basket. I also hang up some of her art on the walls with a roll of tape I find in her desk drawer. She has a lot of good pieces that were just tossed away, crumpled. She's so talented, and I can't stand it when she hates her work. It makes me sad to see masterpieces just thrown away like trash.

When I've done everything I can do to clean her room, I take off my outer clothes and crawl into bed with her, digging deep into the comforter to find her small, fragile body. She makes a tiny grunt when I grab onto her and pull her into a spoon. Then she relaxes into me.

"How was work, Mom?" she murmurs.

"Work-like," I reply.

"It's all so tiring," she says.

I wrap my arms even tighter around her. "It is."

"You should let yourself sleep more." She shoves her butt back as she talks so she's completely cradled by my body. I squeeze her even tighter around her waist. She's so skinny. I know she hasn't been eating, and I hate that, but there is only so much energy I can give to bossing her around. Some days I'm shocked that I even remember to give her her meds. When she's not crashing or crashed completely, she sometimes remembers on her own. But she says the drugs make her fuzzy in the head. The problem is, she has tried so many, with varying side effects, and these were the least intolerable.

"You do all the sleeping for me," I whisper.

She takes a deep breath, and I feel all of it deep in the core of me.

"I wouldn't sleep so much if life didn't hurt."

"I know," I say.

"Do you?" she asks.

Her body is warm. I slip in and out of sleep. These surface dreams bubble up and make everything seem kind of ridiculous and surreal. I dream about Jack walking away, then wake up again.

"No, not really," I reply. I don't know how painful life is. Not like she does. I've always been on the go, making things work. Balancing and living hard so she doesn't have to, so I can protect her from the world.

"I hope you never know," she says. "My everything hurts. I can feel the press of it at all angles. Like I live on a planet all by myself, a heavier planet, with way more gravity."

When she tells me this kind of stuff, usually late at night, I just let her talk. I let her describe the world as she sees it, as she feels it. It is so alien to me sometimes that I don't doubt she's on a faraway planet. Lost in space, a million miles from home. I hold her as tightly as I can, but the pressure of my arms makes me feel like I might break her, like *I* am that extra gravity. I know she sees everything I do for her. It can't be easy living life needing someone to remember everything for you. Just like it isn't easy for me to live life for someone else. I don't resent it though—I can't. I have no place in my heart to hate her. All I have is love for my sweet, sad, beautiful sister.

"I just want to fly," she whispers, her voice getting more and more distant. "I want to live on the moon where the gravity is low and I can just soar."

She talks like this all the time. She calls me the sun and herself the moon. I know she has a dark side that, no matter how bright I shine, I will never be able to touch.

"My sweet little moon," I say, rocking her back and forth ever so slightly.

"Have I told you lately that I love you?" she asks, her voice barely loud enough to reach me.

"Every day," I say. The tone in my voice is a promise that I know she loves me. An allowance for all the times she doesn't say it.

We sink deep into sleep, our bodies sharing heat, darkness and dreams.

Chapter Eleven

When I wake up Jude is gone. This could be a good thing, but it could also be very bad. I sit up in her bed and listen to the radio alarm blaring from my room. I look around for any sign of my sister. Her backpack is gone, and there are a couple of items of clothing strewn on the floor. All my work last night undone by a pair of socks and three discarded T-shirts.

When I go downstairs I see that she's gone gone. But there's a note.

Gone to school early for a sketch class. Pancakes in the oven. —J

I would prefer that she wouldn't leave the oven on when I'm asleep, but I am grateful for the pancakes. Unlike me, she is a pancake master—hers are fluffy, bubbly, delicious things that make me flush with jealousy. More often than not, I can take her beauty, her talent, but the fact that she can make better pancakes than I can is just a kick in the pants.

I eat quickly, assemble a makeshift lunch—leftover peas and mock-chicken fingers—and then make my way to school. The air still has a bit of a chill, despite the bright, cheerful sun. As I approach the front door of the school, I look around for Jack.

My heart is pounding with the faint hope that he is waiting for me, to walk me to class. He's not. A few of my friends are though. They wave me over. We talk, but we're interrupted by the first bell. We disperse quickly, because we're all keeners who like to be on time even though we don't *need* to be.

When I get to physics, Jack is already there. My breath leaves me for a second. He's changed seats from yesterday so he can sit next to me. We don't have assigned seats or anything, but humans are creatures of habit, and we usually stick to the places we choose on the first day of class.

Jack smiles this lovely, wide smile at me when I sit down. I exhale. Maybe yesterday was just a glitch. Maybe he really did have to pick up some stuff for his brother. Just because his brother didn't actually text him doesn't mean anything. Maybe Jack was checking the time. As soon as I sit down, the teacher, Mrs. Ray, starts talking. It makes me sad, because I wish I'd had time to talk to Jack. I guess in a way it's good, though, because I'm not 100 percent sure what I would say.

I pull all my stuff out of my bag and try to focus. But I can feel Jack's eyes on me periodically throughout the class. It's hard to concentrate when my stomach is churning and my knees feel like jelly.

Then, when Mrs. Ray turns her back to start writing on the board, Jack slips me a note. A small thrill passes through me. I try my best not to look in his direction, although I can feel the force of his thousand-watt smile heating me up.

When the coast is clear, I look down at the note.

Sorry about last night, Penny Lane. Are you mad? Y/N

The *Y/N* makes me smile. Are we in fourth grade? I think about circling Y, but that would be a dick move.

Besides, I'm not mad, just confused. I circle *N*, write **???** and hand it back.

I allow myself one quick look at him before refocusing my attention on Mrs. Ray. She's still writing stuff on the board, ignoring the class. People are starting to get restless. They shift in their seats, talking in gestures and mouthed words. A bunch of people are texting. I like Mrs. Ray, but she writes really, really slowly.

Jack takes a second with the note, then slides it back.

I like you, but there's something I have to explain.

I take a deep breath and exhale slowly, trying to still my racing heart. He has a girlfriend, or a boyfriend, or he's moving back to live with his parents. Maybe he's a criminal on the run, and his whole living-with-his-brother bit is just a con. Or maybe he's a chemistry genius, dedicated entirely to his work, no time for anything else. My brain is on fire. *Stop being stupid, Penny. Get a grip.*

I send the note back to him with a few extra question marks.

He laughs out loud, and Mrs. Ray turns around sharply, eyeing the class. We both try to look innocent. As soon as she turns back to the board, Jack shoves the note under my hand. We could be doing this through texts, but note passing is sexier, so I'm definitely fine with it.

Can you meet me in the theater at lunch? Y/N

I try not to smile too hard. I pretend I'm really considering it, even though there is no question in my mind. I have to find Jude first, because she skipped her meds this morning. But other than that I'm completely his.

I circle the Y very slowly, drawing it out.

Then I reach over and slide the note back onto Jack's desk. He looks down at it and grins. He bends over and scribbles something quickly before tossing the note back at me.

Took you long enough.

I respond with two words, trying to be cheeky, sexy, flirty.

I know.

Chapter Twelve

I'm buzzing with nervous energy all through English class. When the lunch bell finally rings, I jump up and race to the pit. I just manage to get ahead of the crowds of kids streaming out of the classrooms and into the halls. Jude is already at our table. She's hunched over her sketchbook, hard at work with a smoke hanging out of her mouth. It has a long bit of ash, and some flecks shake loose when she moves, but remarkably it manages to stay intact, like a horizontal Tower of Pisa.

"What the hell, Jude?" I say as I approach.

She flips the sketchbook closed and tosses her smoke away from her so fast you would think it had burned her. Then she turns to me and flashes a grin. She looks more awake than usual, and it makes me hopeful but wary. Usually the upped dosage doesn't work this fast. I dig her pills out of my pocket and hand them to her. She takes them dry and opens her mouth to show me.

I nod at her sketchbook. "What are you drawing?"

She's usually not protective about her art—not with me, at least.

"It's a secret," she says. She has a sneaky, joking tone. But I don't like secrets. One of our agreements is not to keep them. But I'm so desperate to get to Jack that I let it slide. I don't want it to turn into a big thing.

"Okay, fine. I have to go anyway," I say.

She grins at me. "Going to go see your new boyfriend?"

I sigh. "How old are you?"

She laughs and turns back to her sketchbook, shooting me a little look to make sure I'm actually leaving before she opens it.

I shrug. "Okay, bye, Jude."

"Bye, Mom. Make sure you're home by midnight or you'll turn into a pumpkin."

I don't even bother with a witty response. I'm too busy speed-walking toward the theater.

Jack is waiting for me. Luckily the rest of the theater is empty. We're usually a few days into the school year before the drama club starts ramping up production.

I smile and walk slowly down the aisle. I don't want to seem too keen, especially if he's going to break the news to me that he's seeing someone else.

"Hi," he says shyly.

"Hi."

I awkwardly scramble up onto the stage. And to compensate for my bumbling, I don't make eye contact. Instead I lean back on my hands and look at the stage lights. Jack is quiet beside me, and the air feels tense, stale. My heart is thumping so hard I'm sure he must be able to hear it.

"You know," I say, to break the silence, "I've always wondered what it would be like to perform here. The lights. The makeup. Everybody looking at you."

I glance over at Jack, and he nods. He doesn't look at me though.

"The only time I ever performed anything was the Christmas pageant at my parents' church when I was younger," he says. "I was the star. It was mortifying. I had this huge cardboard star cutout, covered in sequins, wedged around my face."

I laugh. "Sounds like hell."

He's wearing different suspenders today, with a striped, collared T-shirt. The collar is popped, which most people couldn't get away with. On him it looks hot though. I really want to grab him and kiss him, but I stifle the urge. I want to hear his explanation before I do anything rash.

Jack nods again. "It was." He sounds so serious, it tugs at my heart. What happened between him and his parents? Probably something he doesn't want to talk about. He was so honest about his mental-health issues yesterday. I would think he would be honest about everything else too.

"Sorry," I say quietly.

He smiles and finally turns to look at me. "You should."

I frown, confused.

"Perform, I mean. Try out."

I laugh again. "No time."

His smile turns sad. "You should make time. You can't give it all away, you know. Sometimes you have to take some for yourself."

I feel like he's talking about Jude, and I tense. I get defensive about her easily. I need to keep working. I need to keep watch on her. I need to get good grades.

I take a breath.

But maybe he's right. Maybe I do need something of my own. Jude has her drawing. Why can't I have the theater? It's a little late in the game, but that shouldn't stop me.

"I'll think about it," I say.

He looks at me. His gray eyes meeting mine.

Jack's gaze travels to my lips, and all those butterflies that have been beating their wings in my stomach move farther down.

"Good," he says, looking back up at my eyes.

"But you're stalling," I say. "You have something to tell me."

He suddenly looks afraid. He looks away. Folds his hands, then unfolds them. Looks out across the theater like he wants to run away, right out the door. I want to put my hand on his shoulder to keep him here, but he doesn't seem to want to touch me. He's made that very clear. How bad must his secret be to make him look this scared?

"So you know how I told you that my parents kicked me out?" he asks quietly.

I nod, but I don't say anything because I don't want to spook him.

"They did it because I'm trans."

I take a deep breath. "Oh."

"I try not to tell people because… well, for obvious reasons…" He's stumbling over his words and my heart contracts. I reach out my hand and put it on his arm. "But I really like you and I just wanted to tell you in case…"

"It's okay," I say.

Jack is still staring straight ahead. He blinks, then slowly turns to look at me. There is a long pause, so I keep talking to fill the silence.

"Yeah," I continue, "I mean, gender doesn't really matter to me because I'm pan. So basically I like who I like. And you don't have to worry…" Now it is my turn to pause. "...because I like you too." I don't usually tell people I'm pansexual, but somehow I just know I can trust Jack, like he trusted me.

A slow smile creeps across Jack's face, lighting up his eyes.

Then I grab his suspenders and pull him toward me. When our lips touch, I melt into his arms. And for the third time in the two days I've known him, I wish that everything could slow down. Slow down and last forever.

Chapter Thirteen

As if I need any other distractions from school. Now I can't stop feeling Jack's mouth on mine. His arms wrapped tightly around my waist. His fingers running slowly through my hair. I feel like the gravity on my own personal joy planet is so light I might just fly away.

Unfortunately, I get my wish for time to move slower. But it's too little too late, and instead of it happening in the theater with Jack, it hits me in class. I watch the clock on the wall and will it to move faster, but it doesn't comply. So I just try my best to focus on schoolwork and forget the amazing look of relief and excitement in Jack's eyes when we talked.

Finally the day crawls past the finish line, and I race to my locker to grab my stuff. I'm meeting Jack in the pit so we can wait for Jude and all go home together. As in, Jack coming to my place. So we can be alone. In my room. Together.

When I get to my locker, though, I stop short. There is a piece of art paper taped to it, a sketch of my face. Jude must have left it for me. It's a perfect likeness, but as I stare at it, I see the exhaustion in my eyes and the hint of sadness. I've always thought Jude had the monopoly on sadness. But here it is reflected back at me, and it's undeniable. Suddenly my limbs feel heavy. I feel like I could sleep for a million years. Maybe I am tired. Maybe I've taken on the weight of life by myself for too long. But now I have Jack. He's a reminder that things can be light, slow, happy. I smile as I peel the picture off my locker. Then I notice the words written under it in teeny-tiny text.

Penny Lane is in my eyes and in my ears...

My heart sinks. Of course it's a beautiful message, but it's wrong. The order of the words is reversed. It should be "Penny Lane is in my ears and in my eyes." Jude knows better. I grab my stuff from my locker and stick the picture on the inside of the door before slamming it shut and running toward the pit.

Jack is waiting at my table, and he waves me over, but Jude is nowhere in sight.

"Have you seen her?" I ask as I approach him, breathless from my run.

He shakes his head, a concerned look on his face. "Why?"

"I don't know," I reply. "I feel like something is wrong."

"What can I do?"

I pull out my phone without answering him and dial Jude. It goes straight to voice mail. Another one of my rules she's breaking. *Always keep your phone on.* I text her quickly.

Where are you?

I take off at a run toward her school. Sometimes she sticks around to talk to her art teacher, Rob, after class. Maybe that's why her phone isn't on. Jack slips off the table and follows me, keeping up easily. I wrench open the door of the school, my heart pounding hard in my chest. We race past the classrooms filled with couches and barely avoid a couple of kids coming out of the lounge. I scurry up the stairs, down the hall and into the art room. Rob is there, sitting at a desk that's covered in piles of sketches and paintings. He looks up at me, and the second he sees my worried face, he shakes his head.

"She left half an hour ago," he says. He knows everything. He's the teacher Jude most trusts. Mom and I have had a couple of meetings with him to fill him in on her condition. Sometimes he even calls me if he senses something is up with her. "She seemed okay, though. Energetic," he adds.

Sometimes that is a good sign, but today I fear it isn't.

My heart gets even tighter as I turn around, deftly avoiding Jack and picking up my pace. I run down the stairs and out into the sunshine that seems to be mocking me now with its brightness. It should be fall by now, dying leaves and gray skies. That would be better. That would match the way I'm feeling, the hard tug in my chest, the heaviness in my lungs.

"I need to get home," I say.

Jack nods and grabs my hand. He pulls me off the school grounds and to the main road. Luckily it's a busy street, so Jack has no problem hailing a cab. I try to breathe as he slides into the car ahead of me and tugs me in after him.

"Address, Penny," he says.

I give the driver my address. I feel light-headed, floaty, and not in a good way. Everything is blurry. *Penny Lane is in my eyes and in my ears.* It was a message. I know it was.

Time can't move fast enough.

Every red light is torture.

I guess I can't slow things down after all, or take my time. If I let things get slow, I let my guard down, and I can't do that, not even for a second.

Jack is looking at me, his hand in mine. But I can't even enjoy the feeling.

Maybe I won't enjoy anything ever again.

Chapter Fourteen

When we get home Jack stays behind to pay the driver. I leap out and run to the door. I fumble with my keys and drop them, curse myself and pick them up. My hands are shaking so much I can barely get the key in the lock. A car door slams, but I don't bother waiting for Jack. I just push into the house and run upstairs, taking the steps two at a time.

Jude's door is closed. When I go to turn the handle, I expect resistance. I'm having a flashback to the last time this happened. I almost feel like I can't open it. Like I'll have to break the door open again.

But the door opens easily, the smell of her room hitting me hard in the face. It's pitch-black in here. I have to get her to take down those fucking blackout blinds. I flick the light switch, but the light doesn't come on. I didn't change the bulb. I remember she told me it was burned out. Stupid me for thinking she would change it herself.

I run over to the window. I trip over a pair of shoes and swear, then pull up the blinds. The light floods in, blinding me for a second. I turn to the bed. The comforter is in a big heap. My sister is on top. She's naked, curled into a ball so tight it looks like she's trying to disappear. Her phoenix tattoo stands out against her pale skin, blue and black and red from dried blood. There are pill bottles on her desk. Three. Open. I move closer. They're all empty.

Jack appears in the doorway and looks over at Jude, his eyes wide.

"Get me that garbage can," I shout, pointing at the overflowing bin by her closet.

He grabs it and pours the contents out onto the floor while I run over to the bed and lift Jude up, uncurling her.

"Hey, Jude. You have to wake up now." I'm not talking normally—I'm yelling in her ear.

She groans, and I exhale the breath I didn't know I was holding.

She's alive.

Jack brings over the bin, and I bend Jude over it. She weighs next to nothing, but her limbs are heavy in my arms.

"This is the gross part. You might not want to be here," I say to Jack.

He shakes his head and pulls out his phone as I stick my fingers down my sister's throat. Jack's calling 9-1-1. I hear the tones of the numbers and I'm about to tell him not to, but I don't. I've spent so long trying to protect Jude from the world, but I haven't done my job, because here we are again. The gross tang of vomit fills the air as she coughs and splutters. I look away, glance over at those empty pill bottles just sitting there on her desk. A silent monument to my failure.

My failure. My sister. My pain.

"Ambulance. Suicide attempt." Jack is speaking fast into the phone, his voice urgent and strained. He gives the operator my address. Fills her in with more details of the scene. He walks over to the pill bottles and recites the names of Jude's meds into the phone. How did she even get her hands on them? I picked numbers for the lockbox that I never thought she would guess. But maybe I'm too predictable. So reliable I'm unreliable.

I hold Jude tightly as shudders rock her body. I fumble around for a blanket, something to cover her naked body. I taste salt and realize I'm crying—hard.

Crying for Jude, crying for me, crying because I failed at something that shouldn't have been my job to begin with. How could I have been so stupid as to think I could handle this all on my own? Handle my beautiful, depressed sister?

I can't stop crying, and the tears are burning my eyes. Jude has run out of puke now. I check the bin and see a bunch of half-dissolved pills in there. They'll pump her stomach anyway though. They'll take her into the hospital—the place she begged, bargained with me, not to go back to. They will put her on suicide watch, and who knows how long they'll keep her? And I will come sleep in her empty room. I will smell all her gross and wonderful smells. And I will cry and cry and cry until I have no water left in my body and all I am is a dry, hopeless husk.

Jack stays on the phone with the operator but comes to sit down beside me.

I hear sirens in the distance.

I wrap a blanket around Jude and continue to hold her tightly. I never want to let go. Time moves slow but way too fast at the same time. Jude's eyes are closed, her dark charcoal liner somehow still perfect. Like her. Perfectly imperfect.

The paramedics arrive and try to take her out of my arms. I resist. Hold tighter. Scream "NO, NO, NO!" But Jack grabs my arms, the softness of his touch melting me.

He loosens my grip, and they pull her away. I fall into his arms.

"She's my sister," I whisper between sobs. "She's my everything."

I am a lake of tears now. Salt and Jack's earthy scent are all I notice now.

"I know, Penny," Jack whispers back. "And she's the luckiest person on earth."

Chapter Fifteen

Mom holds hands with me as we sit in the hospital waiting room. It's been two days and I haven't been in to see Jude yet. Two days, but it feels like forever. My heart was so broken when they took her away, and I was afraid it would break even more if I saw her. She's been in and out of sleep. They are keeping her sedated and on twenty-four-hour suicide watch.

I take a deep breath. Mom squeezes my hand. My phone vibrates in my pocket. Jack. He's been amazing over the past couple of days, coming to visit me after school and staying over while my mom was at work. I took time off school for the first time in forever and I cancelled my shifts at Java World. And then I slept. I haven't had so much sleep in who-knows-how-long. It felt so good.

I look over at Mom. Her face looks tight. We are both so tired, but we have been talking. I told her how much everything was piling up on me: work, school, taking care of Jude. We both cried and hugged and Mom promised me I wasn't alone. She has asked for some day shifts so she can be there for us in the mornings and evenings. She is going to take over control of Jude's meds, although I will help her when she needs it, of course. And she's using her hospital connections to get Jude into programs and therapy in the out-patient mental health wing. She will still be an in-patient for a bit though, until she is fully stabilized. I hate that, because I know Jude hates it. But we have to do this right. Over the past couple days I have had to come to terms with the fact that I can't do everything, that I have my limits. That sometimes, like Jack says, I have to do something for myself.

"I'm going to audition for the school play this year," I say to my mom.

She looks over at me, surprised. "Really?"

"Yeah." The thought came out of nowhere, but it felt right as I said it. It felt good to say something normal. We have just been sitting here in silence for the last half hour. I am still trying to get up the courage to go in to see Jude.

"I've been wanting to try out forever."

Mom nods and smiles. "You'll be perfect," she says.

I don't necessarily think so, but I appreciate her support anyway. "I need to make time for things," I say.

Mom squeezes my hand again. "I know. You need time for you, Penny." We have talked about this. We both know this. Now I just have to accept it. I've been living for Jude so much, now it's time to live for me.

My phone vibrates again and I smile. I know it's Jack, but I'll check it later. I'm finally ready. I get up and release Mom's hand. She stands with me, but I motion for her to sit.

"I'll be okay."

She frowns a little, but lets me go.

I walk down the hall to Jude's room and pause before pushing open the door. I almost expect it to be locked, but it opens easily, silently. Unlike at home, Jude's hospital room is bright and clean. The curtains on the window are wide open and sun is streaming through it, throwing light on the bed where Jude is lying. She is beautiful as always, but her black eye liner is gone, so her face looks smaller, more fragile. I move toward the bed. I'm surprised to realize I'm shaking.

This is Jude. I know her so well, love her so much. But she has been my responsibility for so long that now I feel like I failed her. I am shaking and trying not to cry at the sight of her, back in the hospital where she didn't want to be.

When I reach the side of her bed I lean over and kiss her on the forehead. My eyes well with tears as I remember every first day of school when it was her kissing me. That kiss always meant more than anything to me.

As I pull away her eyes open and she smiles softly.

"Hey Jude," I say.

"Penny Lane," she whispers.

I told myself not to cry, but I can't help it. I sink down into the chair beside her bed, put my head down on her arm and sob. I feel her hand on my head then, softly stroking my hair.

"She's in my ears and in my eyes," Jude says, speaking louder over my tears.

And I cry even harder because with those words I know that, at least for now, my sister, my everything, is going to be okay.

Acknowledgments

It's always hard to know who to thank, because I want to thank everyone. My incredibly supportive kidlit writing community here in Toronto. My awesome parents, who nourished my creativity. My amazing husband, who has always understood me, loved me and been my caretaker when I need one. Thank you to my friends and partners who fill my life with joy and stories and inspiration. Thanks to the various therapists throughout the years who have helped me through some terrible times. Finally, thanks to the team at Orca for making this story into a fully fledged book.

Star Spider's stories and poetry often explore mental health and LGBTQ themes. Her debut novel, *Past Tense* (HarperCollins), was published in 2018. She lives in Toronto.

Orca soundings

For more information on all the books
in the Orca Soundings line, please visit
orcabook.com.